LITTLE PIERROT

2 Amongst the Stars

Library of Congress Control Number: 2017952233
ISBN: 978-1-941302-61-3

Printed in China.

Sure, take your time...
Hey...

You're not exactly one to tell me to speed up!
Fair enough...

I guess the clothes really do make the man!

A blank page doesn't have to cause anxiety...

Especially if we introduce it to our friend...

Miss Moon has plenty of ideas.

Isn't that right, Mister Snail?
!

Maybe to defend myself... But to pick flowers, I don't think so!
...and that's a problem!

I hate Sundays...

At least
your kept your
weekday hair...

Sure, make yourself comfortable!
The seat! Lift the seat!

Okay, okay... I'll lift the seat!
Now go!

Well I never...

Hello!

Hey!

My name's Emily! What's yours?

Uh... Little Pierrot.

See you later at school, then!
Don't be late.

?

I loooove school!
I love Emily!

Watch where you're walking!

I heard that when there's a full moon, werewolves appear!
That's nonsense! Werewolves don't exist... No more than ghosts do!

What about talking snails, do they exist?
Only you would know!

Isn't it nice?
Yes, very pretty! But she's a liar!

About what?
Well... When you look at her, she looks like the letter C, like cake!

So?
Look, she's waning! She may be a liar... but she's a very pretty liar!

Here... Merry Christmas! But can I keep the wrapping paper?
FRAGILE

The currents are leading us towards the reef of lights!

The light's going to swallow us... Do something, Mister Snail!
I'm on it!

Turn off the light!
Oops!

It's going to fall! The moon is too heavy!
It's impossible for a moon to hang on a string!

Oh no!

There's not a second to lose!
I can feel the pressure!

Mister Snail, I need your help!
I don't really see anything I can do...

Forget all your theories about keeping your feet on the ground!

See Mister Snail...
It works when we forget about Mister Newton!
I still think we should use a stronger string in the future!

If you had a super power, what would it be?

That's it! I got it! My power would be to eat tons of candy without getting cavities!

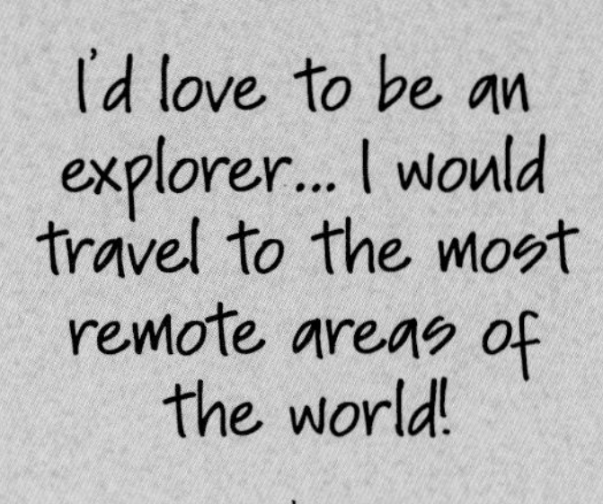
I'd love to be an explorer... I would travel to the most remote areas of the world!

I'd find rare and mysterious objects, either far in the deserts or at the bottom of the deep oceans...

And what if you started by exploring the closet in your room to find your slippers?

I hope she's not jealous!

Don't even think about it!

If you keep reading in the dark, you're going to hurt your eyes!

Don't worry, my friend's got me covered...

Thanks, Miss Moon!

What are you doing?
I'm designing the plans for my flying book!
That idea doesn't stand a chance!
Well obviously the book doesn't stand, it flies!

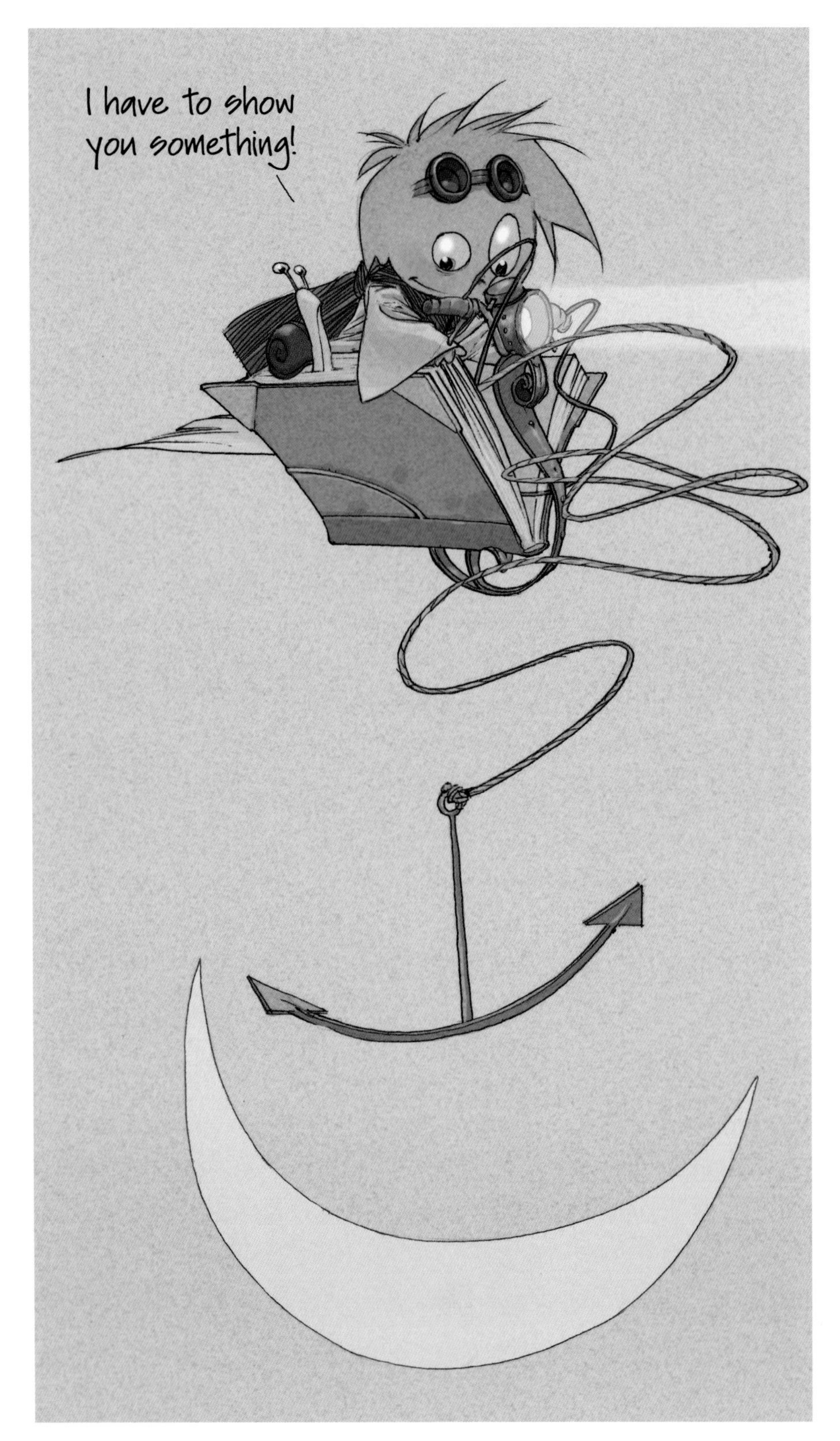
I have to show you something!

And that's how stars are born!

Did you know, Little Pierrot, that Karma is the fundamental principal of Indian religions that believe human life is just one link in a chain of lives, in which the actions you take in your previous lives determines what you are today?

What kind of stupid stunt did you pull in your past lives to become a snail?

Bravo, you're a really magical musician!

You told me that words would fly away, but what's written would always stay...
We're going to crash!

You read too fast! You should take your time and pay attention...
You're right! But it's too much fun!

Pass the tape!

Mister Snail, please hand me the quill so I can rewrite some words...

The book is fixed...We can take off again!
But it's all beat up now...

It's good if a book is beat up...It means it was read again and again!
Come on, let's go!

Huh? Nothing's happening...
How did you spell "flight"?

"Fly" with a t, why?
You better come back to Earth and study your spelling some more!

That's the third time this week...
What happened?

Somebody took the moon!

Some people are too ambitious!

Oh no! I forgot to bring you something I wanted to show you...

I'll be back!
When we lose our heads, we still have our legs!

!

Sorry!
That's clever!

I think we're lost, Mister Snail!

I can't find my bookmark!

Have I already told you about the meaning of life?

...The burden of responsibilities?

Or the burden of bureaucracy?

...The weight of carrying heavy loads?

...Or being hit in the head with a mace?

What did you say?
Forget it!

People always miss the best moments...
Not everyone daydreams!

I see a
pretty pony!

I see a
giant ship...

What about you, Little
Pierrot, what do you see
in the clouds?

What do you imagine...?